Mary & Martha

Dyslexic Friendly Edition

A Message

by

Evelyn Rainey

First presented at
United Methodist Temple, Lakeland, FL
September 8, 2024.

ISBN-13: 978-1-963272-10-9

SheleringTree.Earth, LLC
PO Box 973, Eagle Lake, FL 33839
SheleringTreeMedia.com

Stained Glass Inc
4400 Oneal St
Greenville, TX 75401
info@stainedglassinc.com
Fax: 903-454-3642
www.StainedGlassInc.com

From the Author: I would like to express my gratitude to the people at Stained Glass, Inc for their kindness and generosity in allowing me to use one of their exquisite designs on the cover of this book. Their stained glasses would enrich any home, office, or sanctuary.

What is a "Dyslexic Friendly" Book?

Sheltering Tree Media has taken steps to make our books more friendly for those who live with dyslexia. While the following principles will not make every book readable for every reader, it is our best effort to create products that encourage reading and to support all readers.

Throughout the book, we use a font named OpenDyslexic. This is a free font that is designed to help dyslexic readers distinguish each letter from the others. For more information about OpenDyslexic, how it differs from other fonts, and research behind the font, visit their website: www.opendyslexic.com.

In our books created for adults, we use 12-point font. This size font provides the reader with plenty of spacing between the letters (which is called *kerning*). The bigger, wider font tends to be easier to the reader's eyes.

The space between each word is increased (this is called *word spacing*). This helps better to distinguish when one word ends and the next begins. The line spacing is greater than most common fonts (this is called *leading*). This all should help with readability.

Whenever possible, the text is Left-Aligned but it is not justified on the right side. Allowing the right side of a paragraph to remain *rough* keeps the word spacing consistent throughout.

Our Dyslexic Friendly books are printed on cream or ivory paper which is also thicker than the average book page. This minimizes the sharp contrast of black-on-white pages as well as bleed-through of text from the previous page.

Finally, Sheltering Tree Media has made colored overlays available when you purchase a book through our online store. You can find these overlays at ShelteringTreeMedia.com/shop/dyslexic-friendly.

These are some of the principles we use to create a book as readable as possible to those living with dyslexia. Some may find this helpful; some may not. Please provide us with any insights you might have to improve our Dyslexic Friendly principles. We pray this will enable many to heighten their love for reading.

DEDICATION

For all those Marthas who feed Jesus' sheep through hard work and determination, and all those Marys who keep Jesus in our presence through prayer and worship.

Pastoral Prayer

Dearest God, Utmost Divine,
Holy Spirit, and Jesus the Christ,
We come today to praise your
name and worship at your feet.
We ask you, Lord, to give us
what we need: food, shelter,
belonging, loved ones, and most
importantly, a purpose in your
kingdom. We ask for peace within
our souls as we stand in a world of
war. We ask for the ability to
confer understanding in a world
divided by deceit and betrayal. We
ask for empathy in a world filled
with apathy.

And we ask that You forgive us for the things we have done which were wrong. We ask you to forgive us for the things we did not do which we should have done. We ask you to forgive us for being cowards when you have shown us how to live courageously without fear.

In turn, let us forgive those who have abused us, those who have betrayed us, those who have hurt us intentionally or unintentionally. We especially want to forgive those who just ignored us, as if we were not worthy of attention.

We ask for strength to face what is to come. To stand against the foe and fight for what is true and right. We know that the victory is yours – earned by your sacrifice and enjoyed by all who call on your name.

We ask especially that we recognize the sacred servants and the prayer warriors among us and realize that prayer must come before everything else.

And now, together as the body and bride of Christ, we repeat the prayer you taught us:

Our Father, which art in heaven, hollowed be your name.

Thy kingdom come; thy will be done

On Earth as it is in heaven.

Give us this day our daily bread.

And forgive us our sins as we forgive those who sin against us.

And lead us not into temptation.

But deliver us from evil.

For thine is the kingdom, and the power, and the glory, forever.

Amen.

INTRODUCTION

There were two sisters: Mary and Martha. How many of you have sisters? So, you know how this message is going to go.

John 11:5 states,
"*Jesus loved Martha, and her sister Mary, and Lazarus.*"

This is the Word of God for the People of God:

Thanks be to God.

Part One — Luke 10:38-42
(Running the House)

This portion of Luke tells the story of two sisters who lived in Bethany and had a brother named Lazarus. Jesus is a friend of theirs and visits them often. Martha always welcomes Jesus and His followers and keeps them fed, clean, and comfortable. Mary sits at Jesus' feet among the rest of the disciples, listening, learning, and feasting on Jesus' every word.

In Luke 10:38-42, Martha snaps and yells at Jesus. You know the story! So let's look at it from Martha's point of view.

She goes out of her way to welcome Jesus and his followers into her house. She cooks and cleans and organizes servants to make sure everything is just right. She orders extra food and prepares places for everyone to rest. There's a constant flow of disciples and strangers through her doors and she never gets flustered or upset – until she does.

Scripture doesn't explain WHY she is so upset. We assume she's a little bitter at having to do all the work while her sister just sits there.

It's important to note that Martha doesn't confront Mary; she confronts Jesus. We have to wonder, does Martha want Mary to help or does Martha want to sit at Jesus' feet?

What would have happened if Martha had quit working and just sat down at Jesus' feet? We'll talk about that a little later.

Now, let's look at it from Mary's point of view. Mary sits worshipping and learning at the feet of her Lord. I have to wonder - was this unusual – that she worshipped while Martha worked? Probably not. We are creatures of habit. We do what we are designed to do. Some of us jump into a situation, organize it, throw out the bad and bring in the new; some of us sit and learn and listen and enjoy the moment.

When Martha interrupts Jesus while he is speaking with Mary, she didn't react. She could have. She could have stood up and yelled back at Martha. Or she could have allowed Martha to shame her into leaving Jesus' feet and getting up and working. Or she could have just left the house, turned her back on her family and on Jesus. But she just continued to sit at Jesus' feet: she let Jesus take care of the issue.

Let's look at it from Jesus' point of view. Jesus did not focus on the actions, but on the choices of the two sisters. Martha loves to cook and clean and be the best hostess in the world, and let's face it - no one could do a better job than Martha. But Martha complains. She whines and yells and tries to make Mary and Jesus feel bad for her – for doing what she loves to do. Jesus says,

"Martha, Martha, (notice that He had to call her name twice – perhaps to get her attention) *you are worried and upset about many things,* [42] *but one thing is necessary. Mary has made the right choice, and it will not be taken away from her.*"

The right choice – literally, *has chosen the good part* or *has chosen the better portion;* Jesus is talking about a meal. In today's words, Martha has chosen the side dishes – the food that should accompany the main dish. Mary has chosen the main dish.

Jesus said, "and *it will not be taken away from her.*" He meant, "You're not going to shame Mary into being who she isn't. You're not going to take Mary and turn her into a Martha."

Part Two – John 11:17-35
(When Disaster Strikes)

The Gospel of John brings us back to Jesus, Mary, and Martha at the time when Jesus learns that Lazarus is sick and most likely will die.

The most aggravating thing about this portion of Scripture to me is that Jesus waits. He's been told that Lazarus – his best friend – is dying. But Jesus lingers and only after Lazarus' death, does he return to Bethany. Our sisters react in two distinct ways:

John 11:17-27 – Martha

When Disaster Strikes, Martha went out to find Jesus. She hunts Him down! Once again, she confronts Jesus. Martha blames Jesus for Lazarus' death (Where were you?) Haven't we all yelled at God at one time or another? That's what Martha did – *if you had been here!* I can see her, hands on hips, jaws clenched, tears of anger streaming down her face. Martha debates the meaning of what Jesus said. She repeats what she thinks He is telling her, but she's missed the point. She wants Jesus to do what SHE wants him to do. Although Jesus loves Martha, Jesus remains distant, logical with her. Finally, Martha acquiesces to Jesus. Then Martha goes home and gets Mary.

John 11:28-35 is about Mary

When Disaster Strikes, Mary remained seated in the house. What was she doing? She was praying, mourning; she was living her faith. Romans 8:38-39 states, "*I am certain that neither death, nor life, nor angels, nor rulers, nor present, nor future, nor powers, nor height, nor depth, nor any other created order can separate us from God's favor, which is in Christ Jesus our Lord.*" Mary was not separated from her faith by Lazarus' death.

When Martha tells her Jesus is calling, Mary **runs** to Him – not hunting him down, but desperately seeking him out. She, too, *blames* Jesus for Lazarus' death, but she does so after she falls at His feet. Hers is not the angry tirade of 'You didn't do what I wanted you to do, God!!' Hers was the broken heart and the whispered, 'I know you WOULD have done something else if you had been here.' The whisper of hope and acceptance, still filled with belief and love.

Jesus responds to her sorrow by weeping himself. John 11:35 *Jesus wept* – the shortest verse in the Bible, sums up exactly what happens when we fall at Jesus' feet in our darkest hour, and weep: Jesus weeps, too. Can you imagine, the tears of Jesus mingled with our own?

Jesus follows Mary – not Martha - to Lazarus' tomb.

Part Three John 11:38-45
(Following Orders)

John 11:38-45 brings us to Lazarus' tomb. He's been dead for four days. Martha is already there, and Mary is the one bringing Jesus. Martha and Mary, both at the same spot, but both seeing it through different eyes.

Martha

When Jesus orders the tomb to be opened, Martha objected realistically. "He's been dead 4 days. The smell will be overwhelming." She's down-to-earth, practical, but also, she's following the strict Jewish rules about dealing with dead bodies. When Jesus reminded her of her belief in Him, she orders the tomb to be opened. Note that the servants didn't follow Jesus' order, they followed Martha's.

Mary

When Mary hears Jesus say to open the tomb, she doesn't act. But she witnesses the miracle and in turn: as verse 45 states, *many of the Jews who came to Mary and saw what he did believed in him.*

Part Four — Who Are We When We Meet Jesus?

Pastor Pam[1] has asked that we look at our own call stories. I'm going to ask you three questions:

Who Are You When You Meet Jesus in the Church?

Who Are You When Disaster Strikes?

Who Are You When Jesus Orders You to Do Something?

Luke 10:38-42 (Running the Church)

Who Are You When You Meet Jesus in the Church?

Are you like Mary who performs Acts of Piety — prayer, worship, learning, crying — spiritually supporting the Church?

Are you like Martha who performs Acts of Mercy — cleaning, welcoming, cooking, serving — physically supporting the Church?

Are you Mary or are you Martha?

I know who I am – I'm Martha. I run the Prayer Shawl Ministry and the Senior Adults Ministry and I'm on the Pastor Staff Relation Committee and I count the tithes and serve as liturgist and arrange the ushers and greeters and am on the Preaching Team and eventually – I promise - will sing in the choir. And next year I'm going to be the Educational Director. And you know what? There are a lot of Martha's in this church.

But there are a lot of Mary's, too. Men who pray without ceasing. Women who comfort the lonely. Widows and widowers who sacrificially support the monetary needs of the community. Worship leaders, preachers, singers, musicians, and most importantly, prayer warriors.

I know who I am, but nothing I do to run the church as a Martha will be successful without those Mary's who pray and learn and keep Jesus present among us.

John 11:17-35 (When Disaster Strikes)
Who Are You When Disaster Strikes?

Are you like Mary whose Acts of Piety
include mourning, praying, being in the
moment, being sorrowful, witnessing without
realizing others are watching?

Are you like Martha whose Acts of
Mercy includes leaping into action,
demanding answers, sometimes needing help
to connect the dots between Jesus' promise
and the real world, doing everything you can
so that things run as smoothly as possible
during these times of disaster?

Are you Mary or are you Martha?

I'd have to say, when trauma strikes,
I'm a Mary. (I haven't always reacted to
disaster this way, but I do now.) I pray. I sit
in silence and listen for the Word of God in
the situation. I know others watch me and
learn what being a Christian is through the
way I deal with adversity. I'm humbled by
that. I'm not the one who organizes the
casserole brigade. That's those Martha's

among you. I'm not the one who arranges the flowers or pays for the things that need to be paid. I'm not the one who argues with God, reminding Him that "You didn't do things the way I wanted them to be!" (I used to be, but I'm not now.)

When disaster strikes, are you Mary, or are you Martha?

John 11:38-45 (Following Orders)
Who Are You When Jesus Orders You to Do Something?

Mary, with her Acts of Piety – She runs to Jesus and brings Jesus with her to the place of loss and despair. She makes sure that Jesus is present so that others can accomplish His tasks. She witnesses Jesus' miracle. In turn, others witness her faith and become believers.

Martha, with her Acts of Mercy – says it can't be done, it shouldn't be done (we never did it this way before!) and sometimes has to be reminded of her belief. But then she commands others to accomplish the task Jesus has ordered, and those others follow her commands.

When Jesus tells us to do something, are we Mary or are we Martha?

Part Five – The Divine Duality
(The Church needs both Mary and Martha)

For those Marthas among us, Jesus said that Mary was doing the best thing – worshipping. And I agree. This church is gorgeous. It is clean and smells good. The choir sounds wonderful. The sermons are scripturally grounded and heavenly directed. The ministers call on the sick and provide for the poor and hungry and comfort those who mourn. The deacons serve communion and are trustworthy with the tithes and offerings. The stained-glass windows are sparkly and beautiful. There is enough room in the buildings for classes and seminars and chair yoga and covered dish suppers and groups. The church definitely benefits from having Marthas. But the church is not the most important thing.

Sitting at the feet of Jesus is.

Jesus taught people from the seaside, on hillsides, in the city streets, and sometimes in the synagogues. All the Marys of the world could sit at His feet anywhere. As a matter of fact, Jesus told us that He didn't have a House. We read in Matthew 8:20, "Foxes have holes, and birds of the air have nests, but the Son of Man has nowhere to lay his head."

If you are a Martha or a Mary in this church, then work everything to the best of your ability. Remember, Jesus said to take His yoke: Come to me, all who labor and are heavy laden, and I will give you rest. Take my yoke upon you, and learn from me, for I am gentle and lowly in heart, and you will find rest for your souls. For my yoke is easy, and my burden is light."

Don't worry about what others are doing; do what will help you find rest for your soul. If you find rest for your soul by organizing the Sunday School classes, or arranging the flowers, or running the children's ministries, then do that! If you find rest for your soul by praying for every member of this church and meditating on the Word of God and worshipping with all your heart, then do that! Be the Best Mary or the Best Martha you can be.

It wouldn't hurt Mary to pick up after herself a little, and it wouldn't hurt if Martha took a little break every now and again. But don't expect Mary to be Martha – or Martha to be Mary.

Think about horses that have yokes and draw chariots. (I learned this from reading **Ben Hur.**[2]) If you have them in the wrong place – the Martha where the Mary should be and the Mary where the Martha should be - they pull against each other, and the chariot doesn't move well. But if they are in the right places – the Mary where Mary should be – praying, worshiping, and learning - and the Martha where Martha should be – working, organizing, and serving - ONLY THEN can the chariot win the race!

So, Church, are you a Mary or a Martha?

Are you equally yoked with your sister, or do you tug and fight and pull the wrong way?

That duality, that properly placed pairing, is also seen in Jesus. He is fully human and fully divine. Mary is the divine side of Jesus; Martha is the human side. In this church, we need both the human and the divine, the Martha and the Mary.

IN CONCLUSION

I hope you have been contemplating who you are to this church. Are you the worker who tirelessly pours out time and strength to make everything work well, to welcome and feed and comfort everyone, to make sure orders are followed and all the bills are paid? Are you the quiet one who is here every time the door is open, learning, studying, praying, preaching, being an example of Christianity in good times and in bad whose life is a witness to others? Both are vital to the church, but Jesus said that what Mary does − praying, studying, living her faith − that is the better meal. Jesus said [42] *but one thing is necessary.*

Praying must come before working.
Studying must come before serving.
Living your faith must come before ordering others how to live theirs.
It's OK to be a Mary − a prayer warrior who occasionally steps in to help.

And it's OK to be a Martha — a sacred servant who occasionally sits down to worship. Remember John 11:5 states, "Jesus loved Martha, and her sister Mary, and Lazarus."

Scripture doesn't say Jesus loved Martha because she worked so hard. Nor does it say Jesus loved Mary because she listened to Him. It says Jesus loved Martha and Mary. And Jesus loves you! Jesus loves all you Marthas! You busy bosses! And Jesus loves all you Marys! You prayerful worshippers. You don't have to be both. Let the Marthas be Marthas and the Marys be Marys!

But begin everything with prayer.

The world today would have you believe that Martha served so that Mary could worship. But Jesus made it very clear: Mary sat at the feet of Jesus so Martha could serve.

Benediction

As you leave this sanctuary,
this safe place of prayer, praise, and
worship, and go into the world to
begin your life anew, remember that:
    Christ is with you,
    Christ goes before you,
    Christ supports behind you,
    Christ is on your right,
    Christ is on your left,
    Christ will flow through you in
all that you do.
    Go in peace.

SCRIPTURES AND SUGGESTED HYMNS

Hymn of Praise

Oh Jesus, I Have Promised, words by John
   E. Bode, 1866, based on Luke 9:57.
   Music by Aurthur H. Mann. *The
   United Methodist Hymnal*, The
   United Methodist Publishing House,
   Nashville, TN, #396.

Hymn of Preparation

Prayer is the Soul's Sincere Desire, words
   by James Montgomery, 1818. Music:
   USA camp meeting melody, harm by
   Robert G. McCutchan, 1935. *The
   United Methodist Hymnal*, The
   United Methodist Publishing House,
   Nashville, TN, #492.

Closing Hymn

Lord, Whose Love Through Humble
Service, words by Albert F. Bayly,
1961. Music attr to B.F. White, 1844,
harm by Ronald A. Nelson, 1978. *The
United Methodist Hymnal*, The
United Methodist Publishing House,
Nashville, TN, #581.

Scriptures Used in the Message

Luke 10:38-42³

³⁸ While he was traveling, he entered
into a certain town, and a certain
woman named Martha received him
into her house. ³⁹ A sister named
Mary was hers, who was listening to
his word, even sitting beside the
Lord's feet. ⁴⁰ Martha bustled about,
ministering to those around. She
stopped and said, "Lord, is it no care
to you that my sister has left me
to serve alone? Tell her, then, that
she help me!" ⁴¹ The Lord, answering,
said to her, "Martha, Martha, you are
concerned and troubled with many
works. ⁴² One is necessary. Mary has
chosen the best part, which will not
be taken from her."

John 11:17-27

¹⁷ Jesus came, and he found him already
having four days in the tomb.

¹⁸ Bethany was near Jerusalem, about fifteen stadia. ¹⁹ Many of the Jews had come to Martha and Mary so they could console them over their brother. ²⁰ Martha, as she heard that Jesus came, met him, but Mary sat in the house. ²¹ Martha said to Jesus, "Lord, if you had been here, my brother would not have died. ²² Even now I know that whatever you ask of God, God will give you." ²³ Jesus says to her, "Your brother will get up again." ²⁴ Martha says to him, "I know that he will get up again in the resurrection, on the last day." ²⁵ Jesus said to her, "I am the resurrection and life. Who believes in me will live even if he dies. ²⁶ Everyone who lives and believes in me will not die in eternity. Do you believe this?" ²⁷ She said to him, "Surely, Lord. I've believed that you are Christ, God's Son, who has come into the world."

John 11:28-35

²⁸ When she said this, she went and called Mary her sister quietly, saying, "The teacher is here, and he is calling you." ²⁹ As she heard, she gets up quickly and comes to him, ³⁰ for Jesus had not yet come into the town, yet was still in that place where Martha met him. ³¹ The Jews who were with her in the house and were comforting her, when they had seen Mary, that she got up quickly and went out, followed her, saying that "She goes to the tomb so she can weep there." ³² Mary, when she had come where Jesus was, seeing him, fell at his feet. She said, "Lord, if you had been here, my brother would not be dead." ³³ As he saw her weeping, and the Jews who came with her weeping, Jesus groaned in spirit and was disturbed in himself. ³⁴ He said, "Where have you put

him?" They say to him, "Lord, come and see." ³⁵ Jesus wept.

John 11:38-45

³⁸ Jesus, again groaning in himself, came to the tomb. It was a cave, and a stone was placed over it. ³⁹ Jesus said, "Take the stone away." Martha, sister of him who died, says to him, "Lord, he already stinks, for it's the fourth day. ⁴⁰ Jesus says to her, "Haven't I said to you that if you believe, you will see God's glory?" ⁴¹ So they took away the stone. Jesus, lifting eyes above, said, "Father, I give thanks to You that You have heard me. ⁴² I knew that You always hear me – yet I've spoken for the sake of the people who stands around, that they may believe that You've sent me." ⁴³ When he said this, he shouted in a great voice, "Lazarus, come out!" ⁴⁴ He who was dead comes out at

once, bound feet and hands by cloths, and his face was tied with a kerchief. Jesus says to them, "Untie him, and let him go." [45] Therefore many of the Jews who had come to Mary and seen what he did believed in him.

Matthew 8:20

Jesus says to him, "Foxes have holes and sky's birds nests, but man's Son does not have where he may lay his head."

Matthew 11:28-30

[28]"Come to me, all you who labor and are burdened, and I will refresh you! [29] Take my yoke on you and learn from me, for I am humble and lowly in heart, and you will find rest for your souls. [30] My yoke is smooth, and my burden is light."

Background Scriptures for the Message:

Matthew 25:35-36

[35] I hungered, and you've given me
something to eat. I thirsted, and
you've given me something to drink.
I was homeless, and you welcomed
me; [36] naked, and you've clothed
me; weak, and you've visited me. I
was in prison, and you've come to
me.

Acts 6:1-4

[1] In those days, as the number of
disciples was increasing, a complaint
grew up of Greeks against Hebrews,
because their widows were
considered in the daily ministry· [2]
The twelve, calling together the
multitude of disciples, said, "It's not
fair for us to abandon God's word
and wait on tables. [3] Therefore,
brothers, consider seven men of
good testimony from among you,

full of Spirit and wisdom, whom we may appoint over this work. 4 We indeed will be instant to prayer and the word's ministry."

Matthew 14:16-21

16 Jesus said to them, "They don't have to go. Give them something to eat yourselves!" 17 They answered him, "We don't have anything here except five loaves and two fish." 18 Jesus said to them, "Bring them here to me." 19 When he had commanded the crowd to sit down on the grass, taking the five loaves and two fish, looking up into the sky, he blessed, and broke, and gave the loaves to the disciples. The disciples gave them to the crowds, 20 and all ate and were full. They took up the leftovers — twelve baskets full of fragments. 21 The number of those eating was

five thousand men, apart from
women and little ones.

Matthew 15:36-38

[36] Taking the seven loaves and the fish,
and giving thanks, he broke them
and gave them to his disciples, and
the disciples gave them to the
people. [37] All ate and were full, and
they took up from what was left
over seven baskets full of
fragments. [38] Those who ate were
four thousand men, in addition to
children and women.

NOTES

[1] Rev. Pam DeDea, United Methodist Temple, Lakeland, FL in her series on The Call, Autumn 2024.

[2] *Ben-Hur: A Tale of the Christ* by Lew Wallace was originally published on November 12, 1880, by Harper & Brothers.

[3] All Scripture in this book are taken from *The Latin Testament Project Bible* ©2008-2016, John G. Cunyus

ABOUT THE AUTHOR

Evelyn Rainey has always loved to tell stories and help others understand. As such, she is a published author and educator. But she is also a cat wrangler, and crochet artist, and grows papayas in her backyard. She manages

SheiteringTree.Earth, LLC Publishing and facilitates the **United Methodist Temple** Prayer Shawl Ministry and the Senior Adults Program there, as well as serving on the SPRC and will become the Educational Director beginning in 2025. She is in the process of becoming a Certified Lay Minister through the United Methodist Church. As such, she would be honored to come to your church as a guest minister, speaker, or soloist. Her grandmother always advised her to be "ready to preach, sing or pray at a moment's notice." Evelyn joyfully heeds that advice.

After 38 years in education, Evelyn retired after having earned BS degrees and Certificates of Endorsement in Early Childhood Education, Elementary Education, Gifted Education, Integrated Middle School Curriculum, English for Speakers of Other Languages, and Journalism. She also taught all grade levels from Kindergarten through Adult and at many different facilities, including jails and teen pregnancy centers.

Evelyn has over a dozen books published including science fiction, fantasy, historical fiction, new age urban fantasy, metaphysical and visionary, pastoral handbooks, and children's books. She currently has a list of a dozen new projects she plans to have published over the next few years. She has facilitated writer groups (and continues to do so with on-line meetings and would love you to join them (see the https://www.shelteringtreemedia.com/events). She has been guest speaker and guest author at writer conferences and conventions throughout the southeast US.

Her love of teaching has expanded into videos for book trailers, crochet lessons, meditation series, Bible studies, memorial videos, as well as interviews and writing lessons.
(See her YouTube channel **evelynrainey4780.**)

Evelyn is able to conduct interviews and conferences in person (within a reasonable distance), and via phone and video communication (zoom, duo, etc.) She welcomes questions and comments from her readers but prefers to be contacted initially through https://evelynrainey.com/contact.

DISCUSSION GUIDE FOR BOOK CLUBS, JOURNALING, SMALL GROUPS, OR PERSONAL CONTEMPLATION

1. What were the relationships between Jesus, Mary, Martha, and Lazarus?

_____

_____

_____

_____

_____

2. Have you ever yelled at God? Why or why not?

3. Why do you think Martha addressed her complaints to Jesus instead of to Mary?

4. In your church or family, has anyone
    just had enough and yelled? What
    happened?

    _____

    _____

    _____

    _____

5. In your church or family, have you been
    shamed into leaving what you loved or
    forced to do what you don't love?
    Briefly explain what happened.

    _____

    _____

    _____

    _____

6. What do you love to do in the church?

_____

_____

_____

_____

7. What do you avoid doing in church?

_____

_____

_____

_____

8. In your opinion, has God ever taken too long to answer your request? What was it about? What happened? What did you learn from this?

_____

_____

_____

_____

9. Do you find yourself telling God how you want Him to do things? How can you change *from telling God what to do to believing God will do what is best?*

_____

_____

_____

_____

10. Is God distant and logical with you or does He weep with you? How do you feel about this?

_____

_____

_____

_____

11. Why do you think the servants waited for Martha's commands rather than immediately obeying Jesus?

_____

_____

_____

_____

12. Why do you think Mary didn't follow Jesus' command to open the tomb?

_____

_____

_____

_____

_____

13. Name and describe an incident where you witnessed someone else's faith.

_____

_____

_____

_____

_____

14. How do you feel when someone bullies you to do something in church?

_____

_____

_____

_____

_____

15. In what ways may you have bullied someone to do something at church?

_____

_____

_____

_____

_____

16. How did you come to believe in Jesus?

17. If you do something wonderful at church, have you trained another person to learn how to do it? Why or why not?

18. Who are you when you meet Jesus in the church?

19. Who are you when disaster strikes?

20. Who are you when Jesus orders you to do something?

_____

_____

_____

_____

_____

_____

_____

_____

_____

Earth
Publishing
ShelteringTreeMedia.com

We publish books to help you
feed His sheep.

Visit

ShelteringTreeMedia.com

for more information.

www.ingramcontent.com/pod-product-compliance
Lightning Source LLC
Chambersburg PA
CBHW031903170626
46807CB00004B/1869